FAMILY PETS

OUR PET CAT

by Michele Jakubowski
illustrated by Kev Payne

GRASSHOPPER

Tools for Parents & Teachers

Grasshopper Books enhance imagination and introduce the earliest readers to fiction with fun storylines and illustrations. The easy-to-read text supports early reading experiences with repetitive sentence patterns and sight words.

Before Reading

- Look at the cover illustration. What do readers see? What do they think the book will be about?
- Look at the picture glossary together. Sound out the words. Ask readers to identify the first letter of each vocabulary word.

Read the Book

- "Walk" through the book, reading to or along with the reader. Point to the illustrations as you read.

After Reading

- Review the picture glossary again. Ask readers to locate the words in the text.
- Ask the reader: Do you have a pet cat? If not, would you like one?

Grasshopper Books are published by Jump!
5357 Penn Avenue South
Minneapolis, MN 55419
www.jumplibrary.com

Library of Congress Cataloging-in-Publication Data

Names: Jakubowski, Michele, author.
Payne, Kev, 1978- illustrator.
Title: Our pet cat / by Michele Jakubowski;
illustrated by Kev Payne.
Description: Minneapolis, MN: Jump!, Inc., [2022]
Series: Family pets
Includes reading tips and supplementary back matter.
Audience: Ages 5-7.
Identifiers: LCCN 2020058555 (print)
LCCN 2020058556 (ebook)
ISBN 9781636901954 (hardcover)
ISBN 9781636901961 (paperback)
ISBN 9781636901978 (ebook)
Subjects: LCSH: Readers (Primary)
Cats–Juvenile fiction.
Classification: LCC PE1119.2 .J352 2022 (print)
LCC PE1119.2 (ebook)
DDC 428.6/2–dc23
LC record available at https://lccn.loc.gov/2020058555
LC ebook record available at https://lccn.loc.gov/2020058556

Editor: Eliza Leahy
Direction and Layout: Anna Peterson
Illustrator: Kev Payne

Printed in the United States of America at
Corporate Graphics in North Mankato, Minnesota.

Table of Contents

Welcome Home, Coco!

We got a cat!

Her name is Coco.

"This is your new home, Coco," I say. "You're going to love it!"

Coco meows.

“Will you give her a treat, Tina?” Mom asks me.

I pick up the treat bag. I shake it.

Coco is excited. She jumps up. She wants a treat!

We all take care of Coco.

My dad and sister
clean the litter box.

I brush Coco.

KITTY
LITTER

Coco loves toys!

She chases her ball.

She can jump high!

“Good job, Coco!” I say.

Coco likes to climb.

She climbs up high.

She watches the birds.

It is family movie night.
Coco is part of our family.

She sits on my lap.
She purrs.

I think Coco likes
her new home!

Let's Review!

Everyone in the family cares for Coco. What does Tina do to care for Coco?

A. feeds Coco **B.** cleans the litter box
C. picks up Coco's toys **D.** brushes Coco

Picture Glossary

chases
Runs after someone or something in order to catch it or scare it away.

climb
To move up or down.

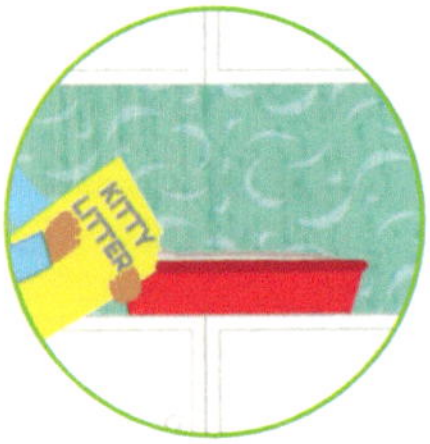

litter box
A place cats use as a toilet.

meows
Makes a crying sound.

purrs
Makes a low, vibrating sound.

treat
A food that tastes good and is not eaten very often.

Let's Review! Answer Key: **D.** brushes Coco